"Within a framework of mutual love a bunny tells his mother how he will run away and she answers his challenge by indicating how she will catch him. Warmth prevails." (Starred Review)   —*School Library Journal*

"Clement Hurd has redone some of his illustrations to make the book an even wiser and more tender odyssey. Warm color and a fullness of form in the illustrations provide a soft security for the wild bunny fantasies."
                          —*The Christian Science Monitor*

THE
RUNAWAY BUNNY

by Margaret Wise Brown
Pictures by Clement Hurd

HarperTrophy
A Division of HarperCollins*Publishers*

THE RUNAWAY BUNNY

Once there was a little bunny who wanted to run away.
So he said to his mother, "I am running away."
"If you run away," said his mother, "I will run after you.
For you are my little bunny."

"If you run after me," said the little bunny,
"I will become a fish in a trout stream
and I will swim away from you."

"If you become a fish in a trout stream," said his mother,
"I will become a fisherman and I will fish for you."

"If you become a fisherman," said the little bunny,
"I will become a rock on the mountain, high above you."

"If you become a rock on the mountain high above me,"
said his mother, "I will be a mountain climber,
and I will climb to where you are."

"If you become a mountain climber,"
said the little bunny,
"I will be a crocus in a hidden garden."

"If you become a crocus in a hidden garden,"
said his mother, "I will be a gardener. And I will find you."

"If you are a gardener and find me,"
said the little bunny, "I will be a bird
and fly away from you."

"If you become a bird and fly away from me,"
said his mother, "I will be a tree that you come home to."

"If you become a tree," said the little bunny,
"I will become a little sailboat,
and I will sail away from you."

"If you become a sailboat and sail away from me,"
said his mother, "I will become the wind
and blow you where I want you to go."

"If you become the wind and blow me," said the little bunny,
"I will join a circus and fly away on a flying trapeze."

"If you go flying on a flying trapeze," said his mother,
"I will be a tightrope walker,
and I will walk across the air to you."

"If you become a tightrope walker and walk across the air,"
said the bunny, "I will become a little boy
and run into a house."

"If you become a little boy and run into a house,"
said the mother bunny, "I will become your mother
and catch you in my arms and hug you."

"Shucks," said the bunny, "I might just as well stay where I am and be your little bunny."

And so he did.
"Have a carrot," said the mother bunny.